HAGGIS AND TANK UNLEASHED

All Paws on Deck

by **Jessica Young**
illustrated by **James Burks**

BRANCHES
SCHOLASTIC INC.

For Lan and Dad, a good pair -JY
For my Mom, let's go on an adventure -JB

Library of Congress Cataloging-in-Publication Data
Young, Jessica (Jessica E.), author.
All paws on deck / by Jessica Young ; illustrated by James Burks.
pages cm.—(Haggis and Tank unleashed ; 1)
Summary: Tank is a clumsy, outgoing Great Dane, and Haggis is a bored, curmudgeonly Scottie—so one afternoon Tank suggests they turn the wagon in the backyard into a ship and play pirate.
ISBN 0-545-81886-9 (pbk.) — ISBN 0-545-81887-7 (hardcover) — ISBN 0-545-81969-5 (ebook) — ISBN 0-545-81970-9 (ebook) 1. Great Dane—Juvenile fiction. 2. Scottish terrier—Juvenile fiction. 3. Pirates—Juvenile fiction. 4. Imagination—Juvenile fiction. 5. Play—Juvenile fiction. [1. Great Dane—Fiction. 2. Scottish terrier—Fiction. 3. Dogs–Fiction. 4. Pirates—Fiction. 5. Imagination—Fiction. 6. Play—Fiction.] I. Burks, James (James R.), illustrator. II. Title.
PZ7.Y8657Al 2015
[E]—dc23
2014041881

ISBN 978-0-545-81887-2 (hardcover) / ISBN 978-0-545-81886-5 (paperback)

10 9 8 7 6 5 4 3 2 1   15 16 17 18 19

Printed in China   38
First edition, November 2015
Edited by Katie Carella
Book design by Cheung Tai

TABLE OF CONTENTS

CHAPTER ONE
SAIL TODAY!

Haggis was bored.

It was too early for lunch.

It was too late for barking at the mail carrier.

And the cat next door had gone inside.

Tank was <u>not</u> bored.

She was reading . . .

and rolling.

Walk the plank, ye lily-livered scallywag! Yo-ho-ho and a bottle of—

Tank saw Haggis and stopped.

Ahoy, matey! You look bored.

I am bored.

3

Suddenly, Tank had an idea. She could turn the wagon into a pirate ship!

Don't be bored—climb aboard! We can be pirates!

No, thank you.

Come on, landlubber! Sail the sea with me!

What sea?

Tank passed Haggis a telescope.

See? Sea!

I see a sea of weeds.

There's treasure out there—I know it! Let's sail in search of untold riches!

We can't sail without sails.

Tank spotted a sign.

Tank taped and painted. She made some sails.

Soon the ship was ready.

The Golden Biscuit em-<u>barks</u> in search of treasure! All aboard for adventure on the high seas!

CHAPTER TWO

AYE, AYE!

Haggis did not want adventure.

But Tank used her best begging skills.

Finally, Haggis gave in.

It was time for some proper pirate names.

I'm Bootleg Bonny. And you can be Captain Scurvy. Bootleg Bonny and Captain Scurvy: the rrruff-est scallywags that ever sailed the sea! Now, give me an "Arrr!"

Tank gave Haggis a captain's hat.

It fit him perfectly.

He felt dapper. He felt snazzy.

Haggis could tell that Tank needed some practice.

Tank felt her face just to be sure.

CHAPTER THREE

NOT A KNOT

Haggis made sure everything was shipshape.

He checked his packing list.

We've got chew toys, life jackets, a compass, a telescope, a bailing bucket, and a whistle.

Chew toys

Life jackets

Compass

Telescope

Whistle

Bailing bucket

Haggis was getting used to being captain. He was good at it.

Tank was getting used to being first mate. But she was <u>not</u> so good at it.

Haggis grabbed the rope.

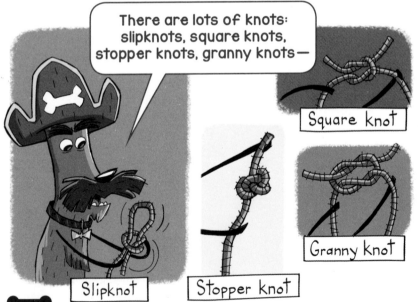

Square knot

Granny knot

Slipknot

Stopper knot

Tank tried again.

Tank kept trying.

Tank was at the end of her rope.

I give up. I guess I'm not a very good pirate after all.

Haggis handed Tank a new rope.

Pirates don't give up! Keep practicing, Bootleg Bonny.

Tank practiced . . .

and practiced.

CHAPTER FOUR
TEA FOR TREASURE

Haggis and Tank wriggled free.

At last, they were off!

They sailed until all they could see was sea and sky.

Then Tank spotted a bottle floating in the water.

Look, Captain Scurvy—it's a message in a bottle!

Tank unrolled the scroll.

What does it say?

It's some kind of funny drawing. It looks like a plate of nachos.

Just then, Haggis saw an island in the distance.

Haggis and Tank rowed ashore.

They landed on the beach and checked the map. The map showed a trail to the treasure.

Haggis and Tank followed the trail over the dunes, around the swamp, and through the jungle.

Then they paused to rest their paws.

Pretty soon we should come to a <u>T</u> in the trail.

I don't think there's any tea in the trail, Captain Scurvy. But I'd love a cup of tea!

No, a <u>T</u>—as in the letter <u>T</u>!

Tank looked for a <u>T</u>.

Sorry, Captain Scurvy. I don't see a <u>T</u>. Or any other letters. Let's just find the treasure and go home. Then we can have a tea party!

Finally, Haggis found a <u>T</u> in the trail.

Haggis took out the compass.

Haggis dug.

Tank dug.

But there was no trace of treasure.

Haggis and Tank tried lots of spots.

Tank was getting hungry.

Haggis and Tank were tired and thirsty. They had to stop digging. It was time to go home.

With heavy hearts and empty paws, they headed back to the ship.

CHAPTER FIVE

TALL TAIL

Soon the Golden Biscuit was making good time.

Full speed ahead!

Then the wind stopped. And so did the ship.

Haggis looked for land.

Aaaaaany . . . minute . . . now . . .

Tank had a little chew.

SQUEAK, SQUEAK! SQUEAKITY-SQUEAK!

They waited . . .

And waited . . .

And waited. But the wind did not come back.

SQUEAKITY-SQUEAKY-
        SQUEAKY-SQUEAKITY-
SQUEAKY-SQUEAKY-
        SQUEAKY-SQUEAKY-
SQUEAKY-SQUEAKY-
        SQUEAKITY-SQUEAKY-
SQUEAKY-SQUEAKITY-
        SQUEAKY-SQUEAKY-
SQUEAKY-SQUEAKY-SQUEAK!

Would you mind keeping it down?

Tank could not keep it down.

SQUEAKITY-SQUEAKY-SQUEAKY-SQUEAKITY-
SQUEAKY-SQUEAKY-SQUEAKY-SQUEAKY-SQUEAKY-
SQUEAKY-SQUEAKITY-SQUEAKY-SQUEAKY-SQUEAK-
SQUEAKITY-SQUEAKY-SQUEAKY-SQUEAKY-SQUEAK-
SQUEAKY-SQUEAKY-SQUEAK-SQUEAKITY-SQUEAKY-
SQUEAKY-SQUEAKY-SQUEAKY-SQUEAKY-SQUEAKITY-
SQUEAKY-SQUEAKY-SQUEAKITY-SQUEAKY-SQUEAKY-
SQUEAKY-SQUEAKY-SQUEAKY-SQUEAKY-SQUEAKITY-
SQUEAKY-SQUEAKY-SQUEAKITY-SQUEAKY-SQUEAKY-
SQUEAKY-SQUEAK-SQUEAKY-SQUEAKY-SQUEAK-
SQUEAKITY-SQUEAKY-SQUEAKY-SQUEAKY-SQUEAKY-
SQUEAKY-SQUEAKITY-SQUEAKY-SQUEAKY-SQUEAK-
SQUEAKITY-SQUEAKY-SQUEAKY-SQUEAKY-SQUEAKY-
SQUEAKY-SQUEAKY-SQUEAKY-SQUEAKITY-SQUEAK!

Haggis grabbed the chew toy and threw it overboard.

50

Suddenly, Tank spotted a speck in the distance.

The speck was moving.

Haggis heard a noise.

Haggis looked. He did not like what he saw.

It's a sea serpent and she's headed straight for us! All paws on deck! Ready the lifeboats!

Swim no farther, ye slimy-scaled snake!

Haggis jumped.

Tank watched.

Haggis couldn't swim.

CHAPTER SIX
A GOOD PEAR

Haggis started to sink. Tank threw him a line.

But help was on the way.

The sea serpent had saved Haggis.
Now Haggis and Tank needed to get
the ship moving.

Suddenly, Haggis had an idea.

Haggis loaded Squeaker into the cannon.

Fire in the hole!

The sea serpent swam after Squeaker
and towed the boat.

67

Finally, Haggis and Tank were back in their yard.

Jessica Young

grew up in Ontario, Canada. She's not a pirate, but she is always up for an adventure — real or imaginary. Jessica loves playing with words and dreaming up stories! Her other books include SPY GUY THE NOT-SO-SECRET AGENT, the FINLEY FLOWERS series, and the award-winning MY BLUE IS HAPPY. HAGGIS AND TANK UNLEASHED is her first early chapter book series.

James Burks

lives in sunny California. Even though he is not a dog, James enjoys chasing squirrels, getting belly rubs, and running around the dog park. His other books include the award-winning GABBY AND GATOR, BEEP AND BAH, and the BIRD AND SQUIRREL graphic novel series.

How much do you know about **All Paws on Deck?**

Reread page 5. <u>Sale</u> and <u>sail</u> are homophones. These words sound the same, but are spelled differently and have different meanings. What are the meanings of <u>sale</u> and <u>sail</u>?

Look back at the words and pictures on page 29. What is the difference between a <u>desert island</u> and a <u>dessert island</u>? Which island would you prefer to be stranded on?

Look back at pages 33–34. What does "a <u>T</u> in the trail" mean?

Why do Haggis and Tank dig in different places?

Would you want to be a captain or a first mate? Explain your answer using words and pictures.